BEAR GRYLLS

GRYLLS

ADVENTURES

THE SEA
CHALLENGE

The BEAR GRYLLS ADVENTURES series

The Blizzard Challenge

The Desert Challenge

The Jungle Challenge

The Sea Challenge

The River Challenge

The Earthquake Challenge

The Volcano Challenge

The Safari Challenge

The Cave Challenge

The Mountain Challenge

The Arctic Challenge

The Sailing Challenge

BEAR GRYLLS

ADVENTURES

THE SEA CHALLENGE

BEAR GRYLLS
ILLUSTRATED BY EMMA McCANN

X Bear
Grylls

This edition published in Great Britain in 2020 by

Bear
Grylls

The Plaza, 535 Kings Road, London, SW10 0SZ

Text and illustrations copyright © Bear Grylls Ventures, 2017
Illustrations by Emma McCann
All rights reserved.

A CIP catalogue record for this book
is available from the British Library.

ISBN: 978-1-786-96015-3
Also available as an ebook

9 8

Typeset in OpenDyslexia
Printed and bound in Great Britain
by Clays Ltd, Elcograf S.p.A.

MIX
Paper from
responsible sources
FSC® C018072

Bear Grylls is an imprint of Bonnier Books UK,
owned by Bonnier Books
Sveavägen 56, Stockholm, Sweden

www.bonnierbooks.co.uk

To the young survivor
reading this book for the first time.
May your eyes always be wide open
to adventure, and your heart full
of courage and determination to
see your dreams through.

TARGET PRACTICE

Chloe held her breath and squinted across the top of her hand at the target.

Thwack.

The rubber band shot through the air and hit the empty can on the branch. It teetered, then toppled into the bush.

"Yes!"

"Five out of five?" Her friend Lily was open-mouthed. "You're so good at this."

Chloe smiled. It was amazing what practice you could get at home with a ten-year-old brother.

"My turn," said Mia. "I can totally do this."

There were still three cans left on the branch. Mia hooked a rubber band over her thumb on one hand, and pulled it back. When Mia let go, the band shot forward – and hit her hand.

"Bad luck!" Lily said.

"Yeah, good try but you had it too far down your thumb," Chloe added. "It couldn't fly over the top like it's meant to. Want to see my special trick?"

Chloe couldn't resist showing off a bit. Just shooting a single band wasn't much good when your brother moved fast. Shooting several all at once, though ...

Chloe got three rubber bands and hooked them over her thumb, one on top of the other. She slid the forefinger of her other hand through them and pulled them all back together.

With one eye closed, she aimed.

"Machine gun!" Chloe announced, and quickly pulled her finger away. The three bands all flew off, *one-two-three*.

It was a good way of hitting a fast-moving ten-year-old.

It wasn't so good at hitting non-moving tin cans. One of them hit a can smack on and knocked it over. The second just made a can totter.

The third missed altogether.

The girls watched the second can, holding their breath as it wobbled.

There was a slightly stronger gust of wind and it fell off.

"That was totally the wind!" Lily complained.

"That was totally skill," Chloe said happily.

Mia checked her watch. "Hey, I've got to get to my Wildlife Welfare course."

"Yeah, come on, Chloe," Lily said. "We should go to the lake – it's sailing next."

"One more ..." Chloe said. She couldn't resist a final shot.

The last can bit the dust.

The three girls set off, when Mia paused and looked back.

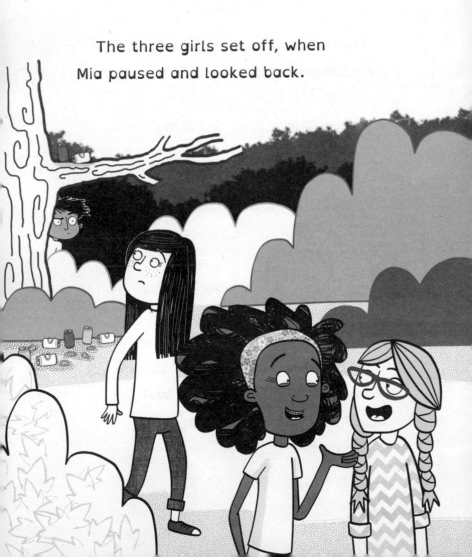

"Shouldn't we pick the cans up?"

"Leave them," Chloe said. "We'll be late. No one will see them there."

The way to the lake led through a clearing where some of the other campers were celebrating the end of the obstacle relay race.

Chloe had been in the race, but she had tripped and hurt her leg, and hadn't run. She'd only needed a bit of a rest to feel better.

Lily and Chloe got caught up with chatting to some friends about how the race had ended, while Mia headed off for her Wildlife Welfare activity.

A boy with his arms full was
walking towards the bin. He'd been
in the race and yelled at her when
she'd got hurt, Chloe remembered.
He dropped some cans near the
bin and one came spinning towards
Chloe. She couldn't resist it. She
gave it a kick back.

"Goal!" she shouted as it hit
the bin. Her aim was bang on.

"We should be going," Lily said, laughing. "I'm desperate for the toilet – I'll see you there, Chloe."

Lily hurried on ahead down the path.

Chloe heard the sound of footsteps hurrying behind her. It was the shouty tin-can boy. She stood aside to let him get past, but to her surprise he skidded to a halt in front of her.

Chloe didn't want to talk to him but he obviously wanted to talk to her. Or yell at her again. What was his name? Oscar? Owen? ... Omar, that was it.

"Hi?" Chloe said cautiously.

"Uh – hi." Omar held his hand
out. "I just wanted to give you
this," he said.

'This' was small and plastic and
round. She took it and saw that it
was a compass.

"Just consider it a gift," Omar
added.

"O-kay. Thanks," she said politely. *Strange kid*, she thought. "It'll maybe come in handy in, uh, sailing."

"Well ..." He smiled bashfully. He seemed totally different to earlier. "Maybe. Either way, have fun."

And he hurried back the way he had come.

Very strange kid, Chloe thought, but she pushed the compass into her pocket and set off for the lake.

Before long, Chloe could make out the silver shine of the lake through the trees. The water was sparkling in the bright sun.

Then, suddenly, she was distracted

by a sound coming out of the bushes at her feet. Curious, she pushed a branch aside with the toe of her shoe.

It was a small baby bird, the size of her finger, at the foot of a tree. Its body was almost featherless. Its head was huge, almost half the size of the rest of it. Its wings were tiny.

Chloe guessed it must have fallen out of the tree above her.

She looked up and could see a small nest on one of the lower branches, and she could hear more high-pitched cheeping coming from it.

"Aw." Chloe pulled a face. She would like to do something. She didn't want any animals to suffer. But then nothing she could do would make much difference, she reckoned. Animals die every day. And anyway, she was in a hurry.

She heard the sailing instructors calling to round people up on the lake shore, and she didn't want to be late.

"Gotta go," she said quietly to the chick. "Sorry."

2

INTO THE LAKE

The dinghies were all pulled up
on the gravel shore in front of
the boathouse. The first job for
everyone was to put their mast up.

Chloe and Lily helped each other
slot the foot of their mast into a
metal track in the bottom of the
boat. They pinned it in place and
sorted out the ropes that would

pull the sail up and hold the boom
in place.

Last of all, Lily helped Chloe
untangle the trapeze. This was
a wire that fastened to the top
of the mast, with a ring buckle
at the end of it that attached
to a canvas harness.

When they were out on the lake,
whoever was wearing the harness
would swing out over the side of
the boat, so their weight balanced
it against the push of the wind.

It took a lot of practice but it
was the bit of sailing that Chloe
really enjoyed. It made the dinghy
zip along.

An instructor checked their
work when they were done.

"Okay," Lily said to Chloe.
"Grab the gunwales."

They each gripped the sides
of the boat and heaved the dinghy
down the gravel into the water.

Chloe was wearing shorts and a
t-shirt, with the harness around her
hips and lower back. The water was
soft and cool against her bare legs.

"Um – forgotten anything?" the
instructor called.

"Lifejackets!" Lily exclaimed. She
hurried back to the boathouse to get
the lifejackets while Chloe waited,

standing up to her knees in the water
and holding the dinghy in place.

Chloe looked casually around. The
lake was a couple of hundred metres
across – big enough for a few dinghies
to zip about without hitting anyone.

Some boys were on the shore about fifty metres away, throwing flat stones so that they skimmed across the water.

A gentle wind whipped the surface up into ripples a few centimetres high, and the sun was shining warm and bright.

Chloe was excited – she loved sailing and the conditions were perfect.

So the wind is from the south? Chloe thought.

She pulled the compass out and glanced at the dial as she felt the wind.

Yup. South.

"Where did you get that?" Lily asked in surprise as she came back with the lifejackets.

"This boy gave it to me. I thought it might be fun to try it out."

Chloe put on her lifejacket and tried to slip the compass into her pocket, but dropped it in the water. The case was made of rubber so it floated. The water was clear and shallow, and Chloe could see the stony bottom of the lake as she bent down to pick it up.

Something glinted below the surface. It was a glass bottle and it had been there for some time, because it had a very faint covering of weed. Small black fish were nibbling it. She thought about picking it up.

"So, are we going?" Lily asked impatiently.

Chloe wanted to get some sailing in with just Lily, before they had to get together with everyone else, so she decided to leave the bottle.

It would take too long to go up
the shore to the bins.

"Okay," she said, "let's catch
this wind!"

They gave the dinghy a final
shove out into the water and
clambered aboard.

Lily took the tiller to steer while
Chloe hoisted the sail. It unfolded
from the horizontal boom and slid up
the groove in the mast. The boom
was fixed to the mast by a hinge
at one end, so it blew around as
the sail caught the wind.

Chloe attached the harness to the
wire.

"Okay," she said to Lily. "Let's go."

Lily pulled a rope attached to the free end of the boom and hauled it in against the gentle breeze. Immediately the sail went tight.

The wind chose that exact moment to blow a gust. It caught the sail and in one swift movement, forced the dinghy right over on its side.

3

CAPSIZE

Chloe was braced and ready for it.

She felt the harness take her
weight as she put one foot up onto
the gunwale, then the other. Now
she was standing on the edge of the
boat, leaning back over the water.

The wind couldn't tip the boat
over because of her weight, and

her weight couldn't pull the boat too far in the other direction because of the wind. The dinghy was balanced.

They zoomed across the lake with Lily at the tiller. Chloe whooped in glee as she trapezed out even further. This was the best feeling ever.

When spray was flying from the bow and the water was zipping past right beneath you, it felt like you were doing a million miles per hour.

They were getting close to the
far shore, and running out of lake.

"Get ready to go about," Lily said.

She pushed the tiller and the
boat began to turn. Chloe quickly
swung herself around the mast.

As she went, she felt something
uncomfortable rubbing against her.
Of course, the compass.

But there was no chance to do anything about it. She needed to trapeze straight out again, as the dinghy started to pick up speed towards the boathouse.

All the other boats were in the water now. A couple had their sails up and were near the shore. The instructor was waving at Chloe and Lily to rejoin the others.

"Hey, let's have some fun!" Lily said. Without waiting for a reply, she changed course towards a row of floating orange buoys the size of footballs.

Chloe immediately knew what Lily meant. They were going to slalom, zigzagging back and forth between each buoy. She smiled.

"We'll show them how it's done!" Chloe braced herself.

The dinghy shot between the first two buoys and Lily immediately pushed the tiller across.

The boat swung around and aimed for the gap between the next two buoys, now leaning the other way.

Chloe danced nimbly around
the mast to the other gunwale.
As she did, she felt the compass
press into her again.

She tried to slide her fingers
down between the harness and her
shorts. Maybe she could adjust the
compass a little if she loosened her
lifejacket? She took off the tape
and then ...

"Look out!" Lily shouted suddenly.

One of the other boats was heading
right at them. Chloe hadn't seen it
because the sail was in the way.

Lily had to push the tiller right
over to get out of the boat's way.

The boom swung around with a
loud *thwack* and the dinghy leaned
over on Chloe's side. She tried to
pull herself up, but her hand was
stuck in her pocket.

At the last moment she managed
to yank her hand out, still clutching
the compass.

Then – *SPLASH*.

The dinghy had gone all the way
over. She felt herself hit the surface
of the lake and water closed over
her face.

Chloe spluttered in annoyance as she surfaced and released the harness from its wire.

The lifejacket lifted her up so that she floated with her head and shoulders out of the water. She couldn't touch the bottom with her feet. Chloe shook her head to clear the water so that she could see her way back to the boat.

Then, *SPLASH* again.

A wall of water hit her from behind and bowled her over. Her body twisted and spun in the middle of a million white bubbles.

Her loose lifejacket pulled free.

And – yuk! Her mouth was open
and the water tasted disgusting.

Chloe bumped into something solid.
The dinghy must have righted itself to
be level again. Thank goodness – she
could pull herself up before she went
flying again. Still blinded by the water
in her eyes, she swung herself back
onto the boat and clambered to her
feet.

She watched as her lifejacket
floated away on the waves.

At the same time, she thought –
waves? How could there be waves
like that on the lake?

And that revolting taste in her
mouth – it was *salt*. The water
in the lake ought to be fresh.

Chloe shook her head again,
then opened her eyes.

The trees that surrounded the lake
had gone. Fifty metres away, a long
beach of white sand gleamed beneath
a tropical sun, and stretched as far
as she could see in either direction.

"Lily —" she started to say in
surprise. Then she looked down.

She wasn't in the dinghy. She was
on a much larger boat. A yacht. White
water rushed around her knees.

"We're sinking!" a man's voice shouted.

Chloe whipped her head around. In the cockpit, at the back of the yacht, a man was rapidly pulling at a rope with one hand as he held the steering wheel with the other.

"Time to abandon ship!" he called, as the water swirled around his feet. "Before we go down with this thing!"

4

FRESH GREEN COCONUTS

Chloe didn't wait to be told twice.
She put her hands together and dived
over the side into the swirling sea.

The water boiled with bubbles.
Her head broke the surface and
she started to swim towards the
beach. Every few seconds a new
wave lifted her up and carried
her a bit further.

Soon Chloe was so close to land that she felt her hands brush the sand. She waded the last few metres while the water seethed around her legs.

As soon as Chloe was out of the water, she could feel the sun starting to roast her through her damp t-shirt. It was like a burning spotlight in the blue and cloudless sky. But that didn't worry her half as much as the question of where on earth she was.

The beach rose up to some sandy dunes and a scraggly row of palm trees. Left and right, the white sand stretched as far as she could see. She turned and stared back towards the sea.

How had she ended up here?

All Chloe could see of the sinking yacht now was a mast sticking up out of the surf at an angle. The man who'd shouted was wading towards her.

He had a tanned, friendly face and wet, dark hair that was flat against his head. He held up a dripping backpack.

"I managed to save a few things that might come in handy. Apart from that, it looks like we're on our own."

"Um – right," Chloe said. She looked along the beach again, trying to see her friends. "But *where* are we? And who are you?"

"I'm Bear, and right now we're a
long way from anywhere." He smiled.
"But I'll do my best to help guide
you back home safely." He smiled
again. "Don't worry. We'll be okay."

"I'm Chloe." She smiled back.
"I really hope you're right, because
from what I can see we've just lost
the boat."

"Well, in that sense, Chloe,
you are dead right," Bear said.

He looked back at the wreck,
and then at Sophie. "But I guess
it also means we are in for some
real adventure."

"You mean, more adventure than
jumping off a sinking boat?"

He ruffled his hair dry.

"That was only the beginning."
Bear looked up the beach. "Okay.
Let's get out of the sun while we
assess the situation."

Chloe followed Bear up the beach
towards the dunes and the shade of
the palm trees.

Bear put the wet backpack down
and started to pull out waterproof
kit bags. He opened one up and dug
out a hat with a wide, floppy brim,
and a cap with a long flap at the
back. Bear jammed the cap onto
his head and the hat onto hers.

Then he pulled out some clothes in
Chloe's size that were like the ones
he was wearing – a long-sleeved shirt
and trousers that looked light but
tough.

"Try these," he said, "while I check out the lay of the land."

A moment later he had gone over the dune. Chloe changed into the new clothes and immediately felt cooler as the air flowed between the dry fabric and her skin. She left her old wet clothes in a heap on the sand.

Chloe followed Bear's footprints, and got to the top of the dune just as he was coming back.

"Well," he said, "we're not going that way."

On the other side of the dune was what looked like a field of tall grass. Like the beach, it stretched away in either direction as far as she could see. When Chloe looked closer she saw it was actually reeds, tall and thin, growing up out of a lake of dark water.

"We can't wade through that,"
said Bear. "It'll be full of snakes
and the leaves will be razor sharp.
We're heading along the beach. You
used to some distance walking?"

"Not really," Chloe said a little
unsurely.

They went back to the shade
of the trees and Chloe thought
of having to hike in this heat.

"It's a shame salt water tastes
so disgusting," she said. "I could
really do with a drink."

"It doesn't just taste disgusting.
It's like poison," Bear said seriously.
"It dehydrates your blood and fries
your kidneys. I've got a couple of

bottles of fresh water in the backpack. But we'll save those for now. There's something else here we can drink."

He smiled and pointed up. Chloe saw green fruit the size of footballs hanging in the trees.

Bear took a canvas sheath as long as his forearm from out of the backpack and fastened it to his belt. Then Chloe watched him shin up the trunk.

He gripped the trunk with his arms and shifted his legs up, then gripped with his legs and shifted his arms. It only took two or three movements like that and he was up by the leaves.

At the top, Bear drew out what looked like a very big kitchen knife from the sheath. He slashed with it and the fruit fell down to the sand with heavy thuds.

"What are they?" Chloe picked one up. It had tough green leathery leaves surrounding a large green nut.

"Coconuts," Bear said as he climbed down. "Exactly the right balance of salt, minerals and sugar for the castaway."

"Coconuts?" Chloe said in surprise. They didn't look much like the dried-up hairy brown coconuts she'd seen in the supermarket.

Bear picked up one from the sand and cut the leaves away, then lopped the top off with several swift strokes of the big knife. He passed it to Chloe.

"Take a drink!" he said. While he gave a second coconut the same treatment, she took it in both hands and peered suspiciously into the hole he had made. A cloudy, watery liquid sloshed about inside.

Well, she knew what coconut milk tasted like, so she tilted her head back and poured it into her mouth.

Correction. She had *thought* she knew what coconut milk tasted like. This was about a billion times better. She grinned.

"Pretty good, right?" Bear said. "You can't beat it fresh off the tree. Now we'll eat the insides too. It'll set us up for the march. I'll chop the coconut flesh up while you clear up."

He looked down at her heap of wet clothes on the sand. "We leave things as we find them out here. Respect the wild and it will respect you."

Bear chopped the coconuts with his

machete as Chloe reluctantly packed
her wet sandy clothes into a bag and
put them in Bear's backpack.

"So, how far do we have to go?"
Chloe asked as they ate the thick
white coconut flesh.

"Well, this beach could go on
for a hundred miles or more."

Chloe stopped eating. She stared
along the sand. The beach had looked
so friendly and cheerful. White sand;
blue sea ...

Now she saw it in a different light.
Hot sun. Salt water. No food. For a
hundred miles.

"Oh," she said.

5

NAVIGATING NATURE

Chloe didn't know how long they had walked already. The sand and sea seemed endless.

The only sounds were the wind and the crashing of the waves. Bear pointed out the high-water mark – a ragged line of dried-up seaweed running all along the beach, left there when the tide went out.

They walked along the smooth,
firm sand between the mark and
the breaking waves. It was easier
to walk there than on the loose,
dry sand further up.

There was other stuff mixed up
on the mark too – bits of wood and
general junk that must have been
washed up, like plastic bags, bottles
and toys.

Sometimes Bear would find
something useful and put it in his
backpack. A length of rope, or a
fishing net, or several good bits
of wood. But his backpack started
to bulge and soon they just had to
leave things where they found them.

Every half hour they drank a little

fresh water from Bear's bottles. They really needed it. Even though there was a whole ocean a few metres away, the hot sun meant there wasn't a drop of water in the air. Chloe could feel her face and her hands drying out.

But even though they only took a mouthful of water each time, Chloe noticed the level going down. She wondered how they would fill the bottles up again.

Chloe's hat kept the sun from roasting her brains, and the brim kept her eyes shaded. But it didn't stop light reflecting off the white sand straight into her face, and her eyes were stinging.

Then she saw a flash of red plastic poking out of the sand. She tugged at it and pulled out a pair of children's sunglasses.

They were the cheap kind her mum might have bought at a seaside stall, but they would do. They were covered in sand, but she washed them in the next wave that came in, then put them on.

"What do you think?" she asked with a proud smile.

"I think you'll make a good survivor," Bear said. "You use what you find, you're resourceful, and use that to keep you going. Smart."

But Bear looked a little sad.

"So ... what's the problem?" Chloe asked.

"Well, I'm just thinking about where those probably came from," Bear responded. "They could have been washed all the way across the Pacific to end up here."

"Cool," said Chloe.

"Only if you think pollution is cool. Plastic, polystyrene, rubber – they don't dissolve. Nature can't reuse

them or recycle them. They just
create waste and cause damage
to the environment."

Then he smiled. "But we can still
use them to help us – and anyway,
they look much better on you than
inside a fish's stomach."

Just then, something smooth and
shiny in the sand caught Chloe's eye.
It was the end of a half-buried clear
plastic bottle.

"So I guess this won't make you
happy either?" she said as she pulled
it free.

"Now that," he said, "will come in handy. We'll take it with us." He put the plastic bottle in his backpack. "Another quick drink, then we need to keep going."

"The fresh water will run out soon," Chloe pointed out as she took the half-empty water bottle from him.

"It will. That's why we need to keep alert and our eyes peeled for a water source."

They kept walking. Chloe felt a lot better with the sunglasses on, but she couldn't help worrying about the drinking water.

Soon Bear stopped suddenly, and pointed ahead.

"Look, there's water running down the bank over there. Let's see if it's fresh water."

They raced ahead and sure enough there was a small stream that wound its way from the dunes towards the sea.

Bear knelt down and put his finger in the water to taste it. And then he smiled.

"It is fresh. We need to make use of this. We might not find another one of these for a while," Bear said.

He pushed his water bottle under the surface and it filled with lots of glugs and gurgles.

"Is it safe to drink?" Chloe asked anxiously.

She thought of the lake water back at the Camp. That looked clear and clean, but they had all been told not to drink it. Animals weed and pooed in the forests, and the rain washed it away, and sooner or later it all ended up in the lake.

"In an ideal world we would boil these in order to one hundred per cent kill any bacteria, but look over there," Bear said. He jerked a thumb at the dunes.

"Remember the reeds? Reed beds are a natural filter. By the time the water's come through the reeds to the beach, it's been washed pretty clean. It's amazing how many communities use natural systems like reed beds to clean up their mess – nature is a great inventor, if you look after it."

He checked his watch, then looked around.

"We can take a break here. You rest, and I'll see if I can spot anything from up there."

He dropped his backpack on the sand, and set off to the high dunes at the rear of the beach.

Chloe strolled along the stream,

down to where the clear clean water soaked into the flat wet sand left behind by the sea. She stood and watched the waves coming in, going out – in, out ... it was very peaceful.

Eventually she turned to go – and couldn't. Something was holding her fast.

She looked down. Her feet had disappeared into the sand – she was sinking!

Chloe gasped and gave one of her legs a hard tug to get it free. Then the other. But both her legs sank down deeper with a loud sucking noise.

Chloe started to panic. She pulled at her leg again. Then the other. Nothing was budging. If anything, her legs were sinking even further, as the sand and mud sucked at her limbs.

In a moment she was jerking her whole body from side to side. Instead of pulling her feet free, she fell on her bottom. She put out a hand to

steady herself, and then she felt
that start to sink as well. She
yanked it out immediately.

Chloe's heart began to pound and
her mouth went dry at the thought
of what might happen. Sinking into
the sand, getting it in her mouth,
her nose, clogging up her lungs ...

"Bear!" she screamed. "Help!
I'm sinking!"

6

CIRCLE OF LIFE

"Stay calm!" Bear came pelting down the dune towards her. "I've got you! Just try to stay as still as you can!"

Chloe trusted Bear but it took all her self-control to stop struggling. She could feel the cold, wet sand creeping slowly up her legs – she was still sinking.

Bear skidded to a halt a couple
of metres away from her.

"You're in quicksand," he said.
"The sand's so wet it can't hold
your weight. Lean forward, and
lie flat on your front."

"What?" Chloe exclaimed. "No!
I'll get sucked in!" She thought
again about getting sand in her
nose and mouth.

"Trust me," Bear said calmly.
"Lean forward so that your body
is flat on the sand. Your weight
will be spread across your whole
body instead of pushing down into
your feet. It'll help the sand support
you, and then you'll be able to crawl
free."

He lay down and reached out a hand. "Look, it's okay. Just crawl across the sand towards me."

Chloe tried not to panic as she lay forward. As soon as she put her hands and arms into the wet sand, she could feel it sucking at them.

But she crawled forward until she was flat, and even though the sand still pulled at her buried legs, bit by bit she felt her feet working loose. She wriggled towards Bear's outstretched hand, until at last his fingers closed around hers.

With one movement, Bear pulled her up and away from the quicksand.

"Good job!" he said with a huge smile. "You kept calm, which is the hardest thing to do. The more you struggle, the more the suction pulls you in."

Chloe took a few deep breaths. Her heart was still pounding and her front was plastered with wet sand.

She tried to brush it off, but it clung to her.

"Just let it dry," Bear said. "An hour or so and it'll fall off."

Chloe just nodded. She couldn't quite make herself speak.

"And I found our lunch," Bear added. "You're going to need some food inside you after that."

They walked carefully around the quicksand and further down the beach. Chloe's legs were shaking but she kept going.

Something white and flat, the size of a tea tray, was lying just above where the waves broke.

Chloe thought that was what Bear was showing her, until she saw the expression on his face as he picked it up.

It was just more washed-up rubbish – a piece of polystyrene packaging. Apart from being covered with wet sand, it looked just like it would have when it came out of the box.

"Do you know how this got here?" Bear asked in a quiet voice. "Someone got their new microwave or TV, but they couldn't take the time to put this in the trash properly."

He frowned. "Polystyrene is so light one gust of wind could blow it down the street and into a stream, then it could float into a river, and then get washed out to sea. So here it is now, thousands of miles from where it started."

Chloe looked at the slab of polystyrene. "But if it just floats, why does it matter?" she asked.

"Because it doesn't *just* float. It breaks up and those pieces block up the stomachs of fish and animals, and strangles them from inside. It absorbs poisons and spreads them wherever it goes," he said seriously.

"Polystyrene never breaks down naturally," he explained. "And it literally kills the ecosystem."

"The ... what?"

"The ecosystem," Bear repeated quietly. "The way all the different animals and plants in an area live together. Plants grow, small animals eat the plants, big animals eat the small animals, big animals die, they decay into the ground and fertilise the plants so they can grow. It's the circle of life – where everything depends on everything else."

Chloe stood there silently, looking at the polystyrene. It looked so harmless – but it wasn't. She wondered how many hundreds of animals could be poisoned by that one slab.

Chloe thought of the rubber bands she had flicked at those tin cans back at Camp – and just left there.

She hadn't really thought about what would happen to them. Would they rot, or would they just stay

there until some animal ate them
and got strangled from the inside?

"But it's impossible to clear all
the rubbish in the world," Chloe
said as Bear shoved the polystyrene
into his backpack. "Even if you pick
up one piece there'll be a million
more bits."

Bear started walking again.

"I once saw a turtle with a plastic
straw up its nose. About this long, all
the way up, with just a tiny bit poking
out at one end," he said, holding up
his fingers about ten centimetres
apart.

"We do good things not because
we can save the world all alone.

We do good things because it is right, and because we can."

"I once saw a seal that had been deformed by the plastic rings from a four-pack of cans," he went on.

"When it was a baby it had got one of its flippers stuck in a ring – and it kept growing. The plastic cut into its flesh, right down to the bone."

Bear paused.

"To that seal it would have made a difference if someone had picked up just that one bit of rubbish."

Chloe was quiet. It was a horrible thought.

Bear changed the subject and pointed ahead.

"Anyway, I promised you lunch. Over there."

She looked where he was pointing.

"Ice-cream?" she said in surprise.

Dozens of small, green ice-cream cones were walking across the sand!

7

UNDERWATER WORLD

Closer up, Chloe could see that the ice-cream cones were shells. Very short, spindly legs stuck out of the wide end.

Bear picked up a shell and the legs vanished. Chloe peered into the shell. Something was moving in there.

"These are hermit crabs," said Bear.

"They borrow abandoned shells because they don't have their own. We'll keep them for lunch."

Bear took out the fishing net he'd found washed up, and a short piece of rope, and folded the net into a bag.

They dropped a dozen or so of the pointed shells into the net bag and used the rope to tie it closed. Then they walked on, with Chloe carrying the crabs.

Eventually Bear stopped walking. There was a cluster of palm trees at the top of the beach and a clump of rocks sticking out of the sea about ten metres from the shore. The sun was almost overhead.

"We should stop for a couple of hours," Bear said. "We'll have our lunch, and sit out the hottest part of the day."

Bear looked up to check that there weren't any coconuts likely to drop down on them, and then they sat in the shade of the palm trees.

Chloe was happy to rest – walking on sand was so tiring and her legs really ached.

"The next priority," Bear said, "is fire."

He picked up a dried-up palm leaf and started to tear it into long strips. "Get all the leaves you can find and do this, will you?"

Chloe was surprised.

"Aren't we hot enough?" she asked.

Bear smiled.

"We're hot, but not hot enough to cook shellfish properly. We don't know what these guys have been eating, so it's best to cook them properly to kill off any bugs."

While Chloe gathered leaves,

Bear sifted through the driftwood he'd collected in his backpack until he found a short, flat piece. He dug a small hole in it near to one edge with a knife.

Then he cut a V-shaped notch in the side so that the bottom of the V just touched the hole.

Next he selected a thin, straight piece of wood about as thick as a marker pen.

"How are you doing?" he asked, and Chloe showed him the leaf strips that she had made.

Bear piled them all together, then laid a couple of larger pieces of wood on top of them.

Last of all he put the flat piece of wood on the sand, with the notch right up close to the strips of palm leaf.

Bear then spat in his palms, and smiled when he saw Chloe's disgusted look.

"It will help protect against friction blisters," he said.

Bear held the thin stick flat between his hands, and put the tip of the stick into the hole. Then he started to rub his hands back and forth so that the stick began to spin in the hole.

"This is a fire drill," he said as Chloe watched in fascination.

"The friction of the drill tip is going to create heat. It will start charring the base plate, and then the embers will drop through the V into these strips of husk."

"Cool!" Chloe replied quietly.

"Then, when we have enough embers, I need you to crouch down and blow very, very gently ..."

He kept spinning as he spoke, working his hands up and down the drill stick.

Before long, thin tendrils of smoke started to drift out of the hole. The tip of the drill had ground up a small layer of the wood into powder that glowed red.

"Now, blow," Bear said. "Gently."

Chloe crouched down low and blew
the embers towards the palm strips.
The red glow spread slowly along
them and the smell of burning grew
stronger.

Somewhere in the pile there was
a loud *snap*. Even though Chloe
couldn't see any flames yet, the
air started to shimmer with heat.

And then it happened. The smoke
and heat did their job and suddenly
the bundle of dried husk burst into
flames.

"We have fire!" Chloe said,
sounding so proud of herself.
"Are we cooking the crabs now?"

"Almost," Bear said. "But there's one more job first, while I build the fire up ..."

He pulled out the plastic bottle that Chloe had picked up earlier.

Five minutes later, Chloe was wading out to the rocks that stuck out of the sea. The sand under the water was soft and comfortable between her toes. She had the net bag tied around one arm, and she carried the bottom half of the bottle that Bear had sliced in two with his knife.

The rocks were a little taller than she was and she half swam, half walked. The waves had died down and the sea just rippled around her.

Chloe pushed the half-bottle into the water and looked through it, as Bear had told her to.

"Wow!" she murmured.

It was like wearing a face-mask to look at a new world. The bottle pushed through the surface and let Chloe see everything below crystal clear.

Above the water, the rocks were bare and dry. Below the water it was completely different.

Small fish moved in and out of seaweed that waved gently in the current. A crab spooked and withdrew into a crevice. Sea anemones were like blobs of red jelly that stuck to the rock, their tentacles flowing.

Chloe noticed a cluster of sea urchins — small black balls, covered with spines like razor-sharp needles. Bear had warned her to stay well away from them.

Bear had asked Chloe to look for mussels — grey-blue shells clinging to the rocks. She found

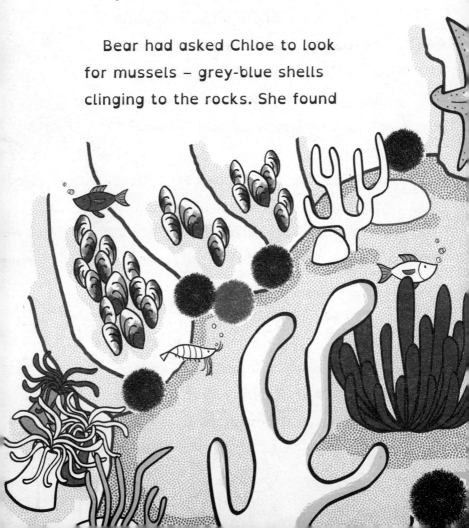

a bunch clustered under a ledge, and
was about to reach for them, when
suddenly she stopped and looked
again through her bottle.

"It's like a whole different world,"
she said out loud.

It was – what was the word Bear had used? – an ecosystem. Everything on these rocks was in balance. If one part died, everything would die. The rocks were all they had, so they all had to survive together.

Chloe saw why Bear cared so much about the rubbish floating in the sea. The whole planet was like these rocks. If the balance was upset, then there was nowhere else for everything living here to go.

She stared at it in wonder for a little while longer, before she remembered her job.

Bear had told Chloe only to get a handful of mussels, not to take the lot.

She understood why now. Taking them all would be bad for the ecosystem. So she reached under the water and pulled a few shells loose, put them in the net and started to wade back to the beach.

Suddenly a spear of red-hot agony shot up through her foot. She stumbled. When she tried to put her foot down again she screamed. It hurt more than anything she had ever known.

Her shouts caught Bear's attention and he came running down to the shore. Chloe blinked back tears of pain as she sat in the shallows and lifted her foot out of the water.

An urchin clung to her like a ball of spiky fire.

Several of its spines were stuck into the sole of her foot and her skin was starting to darken around it.

8

EGGS FOR DINNER

Bear came splashing through the
shallows towards Chloe. He saw
in a moment what had happened.

"Ow. Sea urchin. That's going
to hurt."

He lifted Chloe up and carried
her back towards the shade at
the top of the beach.

"My foot's going black," Chloe gasped through gritted teeth. She had to grind them together to stop herself whimpering. It hurt *so much*.

"Don't worry. That's just the sea urchin's natural dye," Bear replied. "The spines hurt because they go so far in, so quickly. They're *extremely* sharp. But not poisonous."

Bear set her down beneath the trees, then gently lifted her foot up and studied it.

"The bad thing about urchins is that the spines have hooks at the end, so I can't just pull them out again without tearing your flesh. But I'm going to do what I can."

Bear picked up a stick and used it to knock the urchin gently. Chloe heard a couple of faint snapping sounds as the spines broke and the urchin fell to the sand.

"That'll stop any more going in, but there's still five or six snapped-off spines stuck in you."

He made sure Chloe was sat comfortably against the tree trunk and then held her foot carefully.

"The good news is they're just natural calcium carbonate, like your bones. So your body won't try to reject them. They'll just dissolve naturally. The bad news ..." He pulled a face. "It'll take time. Days, probably."

Chloe groaned as she thought of all the miles of beach they still had to walk, and how much the spines hurt when she put her foot down.

"I can't sit here for days!" she replied.

An idea struck her. "Maybe if you made a crutch out of a piece of wood, I could keep the weight off my foot and sort of hobble along?"

"Yes. Maybe," Bear said. "But let me treat it properly first."

Bear got his water bottle and
trickled a little fresh, clean water
over Chloe's foot. Then he wrapped
a bandage from his backpack gently
around it.

"Next step is to see if I can find
something antiseptic to prevent
infection. And for you, the best
way to take your mind off the
pain is to keep busy ..."

Bear dug a metal pot out of his backpack and set it on the sand. Then he picked a hermit crab out of the net bag and held it out to her.

"We need to cook these before we eat them. Blow gently into the end."

Puzzled, Chloe pursed her lips and did as Bear said.

She blew into the opening in the shell, and a set of spindly, armoured legs started to emerge. As soon as she stopped blowing, the legs pulled back into the shell.

Bear laughed, and blew into the shell himself.

The crab started to come out again, and this time Bear kept blowing until Chloe could see its body. It had a puny little body and one big claw.

"They only have room for one claw in there," Bear said, "and it's the only bit with enough meat worth eating. Boil them in some seawater, and then you can get them out of the shells."

He filled up the metal pot with water and placed it on the fire. Then he handed her the knife, sheath first.

"Here. You're in charge of dinner. Cook the mussels along with the crabs. Any that don't close up when you tap them, throw them away. We don't want food poisoning."

Then he headed over the dunes, while Chloe considered the hermit crabs. She blew again into one of the shells.

It wasn't as easy as Bear had made it look to get them to emerge completely.

As soon as the water boiled she threw the crabs in the pot with the mussels. Then she drained off the water carefully – and once the shells had cooled down she used the knife to lever the cooked meat out of the shell.

It took some time to get the hang of it, but she had half a coconut shell full of crabmeat and mussels by the time Bear came back.

"Good work, you!" he exclaimed, before holding up a slab of brown tree bark. "I found a cinnamon tree!"

"Cinnamon?" Chloe exclaimed. "Like, for cooking?"

"Yes," Bear said. "It's a natural anti-inflammatory and anti-microbial.

So it'll calm your foot down, and kill off any nasties that got in."

He took a metal cup from his backpack and began to slice thin shreds of the bark into it. Then he poured some fresh water into the cup, and set it on the fire.

Once it had boiled for a bit, he let it cool then washed Chloe's throbbing foot with it. Then he bandaged it back up.

After that he split the urchin open with his knife, and levered out the smelly mess of its guts. Then he scooped out a glistening mass of small pink blobs.

"Urchin eggs to go with our meal!"

And the meal wasn't bad, Chloe
decided. The eggs were salty, and
the cooked crabs and mussels tasted
good. They washed it all down with
more coconut milk, which was like
dessert.

They sat on either side of the
fire. Bear had his back to the beach,
and Chloe was leaning against the
palm tree, facing the sea.

"We'll stay put today," Bear said.
"I'll make you a simple crutch to
support your foot and you can get
used to using it – but meanwhile,
take it easy, and give your foot
a chance to heal."

"I'll make up a bed for you out of
palm leaves to keep you off the sand
tonight," he went on. "Some of the
spines might even work themselves
out of your skin by tomorrow."

Chloe tried to be brave. The cinnamon had probably done some good but the fact was her foot still throbbed with pain. And she hadn't realised just how much the walk had taken out of her.

She was going to close her eyes and rest when ...

Chloe saw something. She squinted into the sun, then leaned across to see past Bear.

She was right. There was something. There was a dark blob on the sea, maybe half a mile away.

"Bear, there's a boat!"

9

SMOKE SIGNAL

Bear shot to his feet.

"Quick! The fire."

"We've got a fire," Chloe replied
frantically, and a little confused.

"We need a bigger one. To make
smoke to catch the boat's attention.
Lots and lots of it."

Bear looked around. Then he got his knife out and shinned up the nearest tree, the way he had before.

But this time the blade flashed at the roots of the leaves. One by one, palm leaves started to fall down on Chloe.

"Put them on the fire carefully," Bear called. "Add two or three at a time."

Chloe fed the leaves into the fire, while Bear continued to cut down more from above.

The smoke grew thicker. Chloe quickly had to scoot around to the far side so that it didn't blow in her face.

She kept on adding leaves and
the smoke turned into a thick, grey
column that rose high up into the
air.

"Perfect." Bear clambered back
down and helped her put more leaves
on. "Dead leaves burn hot and fast,
but fresh green leaves still have
plenty of water in them, so they
don't burn as well."

"They make smoke instead?"
Chloe guessed.

"Exactly. Which these are doing
nicely."

Bear leaned back to look up at
the smoke. "You carry on here –
I'll see if I can get their attention."

He ran down to the edge of the
water and started waving his arms in
a big wide, rhythmical pattern towards
the boat.

"Hey!" he shouted at the boat.
"Hey!"

Chloe kept her eyes fixed on the boat. It wasn't big, less than ten metres long. There was a small cabin at one end and she could hear the putt-putt-putt of a little engine.

Had anyone on board seen Bear? It was impossible to tell at this distance.

Chloe held her breath as she stared out to sea. Even the pain in her foot didn't seem to matter now.

Then she remembered she still
had her job to do, and quickly
went back to putting leaves on
the fire.

When she looked up, she blinked.
Had she imagined it, or ...?

Yes! The boat was turning towards
the beach!

They had been seen.

Bear hurried back to her.

"We'll have to swim out," he said, "so they don't run aground."

Chloe pulled herself to her feet as Bear kicked sand over the fire to put it out, and gathered up their few things. He stuck the polystyrene into his backpack.

"What goes around comes around. Let's not leave this here. We do something good for the ecosystem and maybe we get rescued in return," he said with a smile.

Chloe kept her hurt foot off the sand as much as she could, as Bear helped her walk down to the sea. The first waves broke around her knees.

After that, she could swim without
putting any pressure on her foot
at all.

The fishing boat had come to
a halt about twenty metres away.
Two men stood on deck, waving
and shouting encouragement.

As they got further from the beach, the waves got ever stronger.

"Keep going, Chloe," Bear shouted. "You are doing so well. Never give up!"

Chloe felt the water lift her up and drop her down again, once, twice. Ahead of her the boat suddenly got lifted up by a bigger than usual wave.

Then the boat was hidden from view as the wave kept coming at her. Chloe saw the top of it begin to break into foam. She put her head down and held her breath.

The wave broke right on top of her. A roaring mass of bubbles came crashing down onto her head.

This time she was prepared for it and
kept her body straight as the current
battered her body. Then it passed.

She lifted her head up. Water
streamed down her face and blinded
her for a moment.

"Chloe! Almost there. Hold your hand out."

Chloe felt her hand knock something hard. She stretched out to hang on to the side of the boat with both hands and shook the water out of her eyes.

She was looking straight into Lily's smiling face.

10

WILDLIFE WELFARE

"Whoops!" Lily said. "I didn't even see that boat until it was too late!"

"What?"

Chloe looked around. She was back in the lake at Camp, holding on to the side of the sailing dinghy. No sign of Bear, or fishing boats, or waves. Her foot felt fine.

The instructor was calling them over to the shore.

"Come on," said Lily. "We'd better get going."

Feeling slightly dazed, Chloe pulled herself into the dinghy.

"Don't forget your lifejacket," Lily said. "It must have come undone."

Chloe reached down to adjust her lifejacket, and felt something digging into her side. The compass was underneath it.

She pulled it out, and for a moment it looked again like there were five directions on the dial.

When she blinked, the compass was back to the normal four directions. It must have been water in her eyes.

Lily steered them back to the boathouse while Chloe's mind still spun.

It all seemed so impossible. But Chloe remembered being on the beach for most of a day, though Lily obviously didn't think any time had passed at all.

By the time they reached the shore, Chloe had told herself it must have all been a strange kind of daydream.

The sun came out and sparkled off the water. Chloe winced and shaded her eyes with her hand.

"At least you've got those silly sunglasses!" Lily laughed.

Chloe grabbed the plastic sunglasses tucked into the neck of her t-shirt. She put them on ...

Sunglasses?

She snatched them off again and stared at them.

Bright red plastic, slightly clouded with salt stains.

It was the pair she had found on the beach with Bear! She had never seen them before today.

So, the beach had been real after all.

The rest of the sailing session was a blur to Chloe. At the end of it, she honestly couldn't remember anything they had done. As they put their lifejackets away, her thoughts were still full of her trek along a tropical beach.

"I'm going to head up to the shop," Lily said, "get something to drink – you coming?"

"Uh – yeah," Chloe said. "I'll catch you up."

There was a bin next to the boathouse surrounded by dropped wrappers and cans. As Lily hurried off, Chloe thought of Bear, and carefully picked up each piece and popped them into the bin.

Then she set off back up the path.

She smiled to herself. *Bear would be happy, at least,* she thought.

At the same time, she heard a boy shouting behind her.

"Hey! No! Cut it out! Cut it out!"

Chloe could hear real fear in his voice. She looked up.

She had seen the boys earlier, skimming stones across the lake. Now a couple of them were laughing and dragging another boy by his arms down to the water. He was struggling to get free.

"Oi! Lads!" an instructor called across to them. "Knock it off!"

The laughing boys reluctantly let go. The boy immediately leapt back from the water and Chloe could see he was upset. He stormed off up the path. The others looked too embarrassed to follow him.

The boy was walking so fast he soon caught Chloe up. He gave her a sideways sort of bashful look.

"Sorry about that. They're friends, really. I just ..." He stopped.

"Hey, it's fine. I get it. We all have things we're nervous of, it's fine," Chloe said.

He smiled back and they started to walk together.

"I dunno. It's just water. I kind of freak out. It's stupid, I guess." He smiled at her. "I'm Jack, by the way."

"I'm Chloe." Before she could say any more, they both heard a faint, high-pitched cheeping.

"What's that noise?" Jack said.

They were standing under the tree where Chloe had seen the chick that had fallen from its nest. *It must be down here somewhere.* She knelt and moved the branches aside. There it was. It hadn't gone far.

"Oh, the poor thing!" Jack said, crouching to look at it.

Chloe looked at Jack and the chick, and remembered how she had told herself before that nothing she could do would make much difference in the big scheme of things.

But then she had met Bear.

She thought of the turtle and the seal Bear had mentioned.

"We've got to help it," she said.

Then she had a brainwave – Mia had been doing Wildlife Welfare instead of sailing for this afternoon's activity!

"Jack, do you know any of the Wildlife Welfare leaders?" she asked.

"Could you go and find one? I'll stay here and guard it, and make sure a cat or something doesn't get it."

"Sure."

Jack quickly ran off back to Camp.

While Chloe watched over the chick and waited, she thought about Jack. She felt a bit sorry for him – having friends push him like that, yet also missing out on all the fun he could have if he could swim.

Chloe wondered what Bear would say to Jack, if he was here.

Jack came back after a couple of minutes with the woman who ran the Camp's Wildlife Welfare course.

She was carrying a folding ladder and other bits of kit.

Chloe showed her the chick on the ground.

"Now, let's see this nest."

The woman unfolded the ladder and attached it to the branch where the nest was. Then she carefully climbed the ladder, whilst Chloe gently picked the chick up.

Chloe passed it up to the lady, who tipped it back into the nest. Then she smiled down at Chloe.

"Well done! There's three of them up here. The mother might come back, so we'll leave them where it's safe and not interfere too much. Sometimes humans can make things worse not better. But we'll keep an eye on them in case she doesn't return."

The woman climbed back down again and folded up the ladder. She gave Chloe a smile.

"You're not in my Wildlife Welfare group, are you? Well, I think you've earned a badge anyway. I'll see you get one."

Chloe blinked. She really hadn't expected to get a badge. She had just been doing what was right. Making a difference in the small things.

The woman headed off back to Camp. Chloe and Jack walked after her.

"Well done," Jack said with a smile.

"Thanks. I wasn't expecting a badge! What's really weird is, this morning I wouldn't have cared."

Jack looked interested at her honesty.

"So what changed?"

Chloe laughed nervously.

"I met ..." She stopped, and bit her tongue. She had been going to tell Jack about Bear, but how could she? He'd think she was mad.

But then suddenly Chloe was absolutely certain Bear could help Jack with his fear of water. After all, he had helped her, and she hadn't even realised she had a problem until then.

She still had the compass in her pocket.

Chloe took it out and looked thoughtfully at it. She remembered she had seen five directions on it, but now it just had four. But Chloe was sure the compass had something to do with meeting Bear.

"Oh, cool," Jack said. "A compass. Can I see?"

"Sure."

She passed it over to Jack.

"Actually, you can keep it," she said. "Just consider it a gift."

The End

Bear Grylls got the taste for adventure at a young age from his father, a former Royal Marine. After school, Bear joined the Reserve SAS, then went on to become one of the youngest ever people to climb Mount Everest, just two years after breaking his back in three places during a parachute jump.

Amongst other adventures he has led expeditions to the Arctic and the Antarctic, crossed oceans and set world records in skydiving and paragliding.

Bear is also a bestselling author and the host of television programmes such as *Survival School* and *The Island*.

He has shared his survival skills with people all over the world, and has taken many famous movie stars and sports stars on adventures – and even President Barack Obama!

Bear Grylls is Chief Scout to the UK Scouting Association, encouraging young people to

have great adventures, follow
their dreams and to look after
their friends. Bear is also honorary
Colonel to the Royal Marine
Commandos.

When Bear's not travelling the
world, he lives with his wife and
three sons on a barge in London,
or on an island off the coast of
Wales.

Find out more at
www.beargrylls.com

TEST YOUR SEA
SURVIVAL KNOWLEDGE!

1 Why shouldn't you drink seawater?

a) it tastes disgusting

b) it will dehydrate you

c) fish wee in it

2 Where is the best place to walk on the beach?

a) along the seashore, paddling in the surf

b) In the dry sand, so you don't get wet

c) between the high water mark and the shoreline, on firm sand

3 You're stuck in quicksand and sinking! What do you do?

a) lie forward and put your whole body down

b) use your hands to dig your feet out

c) wriggle and pull as hard as you can

4 How can you attract the attention of a boat sailing past?

a) swim out towards it

b) climb a palm tree

c) make thick smoke from a fire

Answers

1: b) Seawater is very salty and makes your body dry out quickly, which is dangerous.

2: c) It's very tiring to walk on both loose dry sand or in water. Stick to firm sand to save energy.

3: a) You won't sink as fast if you spread your weight flat on the sand, so lie down and then pull your legs out.

4: c) Smoke will rise up so the boat can see where you are on the beach – you won't be visible in the water or up a tree.

DID YOU KNOW?

- Hermit crabs have to get new shells as they grow bigger. Sometimes they exchange them with other crabs ... and sometimes they fight over shells!

- Coconuts are not just good for eating and drinking. Coconut leaves can build a fire, be made into brooms or thatch for roofs, or woven into mats. Everything you need for island survival!

•Sea urchins are also called 'sea hedgehogs' because of their spiky appearance. Their spines protect their delicate insides, which are delicious to other marine predators ... and humans. In many countries sea urchins are an expensive delicacy.

This brilliant **Bear Grylls Adventure** is set in a reader-friendly font and design, for maximum enjoyment for everyone.

The font we have used is called OpenDyslexic. You can find out more about it here: **www.opendyslexic.org**

Dyslexia affects as many as 1 in 10 people, and often makes reading more difficult. We wanted to make our books as easy to enjoy as possible, so this special font and a design with lots of space helps us do just that.

Not everyone with difficulty reading has dyslexia, and not everyone with dyslexia has the same difficulties. You can find out more about dyslexia on these wonderful websites:

The Dyslexia Association: **dyslexia.uk.net**

British Dyslexia Assocation: **bdadyslexia.org.uk**

Dyslexia Scotland: **www.dyslexiascotland.org.uk**

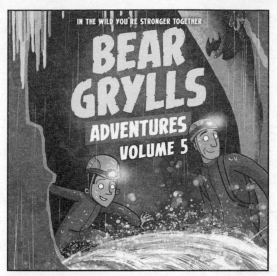

Cave Challenge & Mountain Challenge

Arctic Challenge & Sailing Challenge

Available at all audiobook retailers

THE BEAR GRYLLS

ADVENTURES SERIES

THE SEA CHALLENGE

THE RIVER CHALLENGE

THE EARTHQUAKE CHALLENGE

THE MOUNTAIN CHALLENGE

THE ARCTIC CHALLENGE

THE SAILING CHALLENGE

FOR MORE INFORMATION ON
BEAR GRYLLS, CHECK OUT

beargrylls.com